D1247111

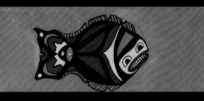

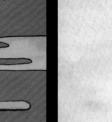

Brothers
of the WOLF

Written and Illustrated
by Caroll Simpson

H
HERITAGE

VICTORIA | VANCOUVER | CALGARY

A woman went walking in the forest and found two wolf cubs. She took them home and raised them as her own sons.

The woman cared for the two brothers and taught them the ways of the First People.

One day, as he was soaring over a thick blanket
of forest, Raven came across a mighty river dividing
a massive wilderness. He followed it to the Pacific
Ocean. Along the shore, Raven looked down to see
a small village of the First People. Two wolves, one
black and one white, were romping along the beach.

As the sun set, the two brothers of the Wolf, T'kope and Klale, started homeward. Mother had taught the boys to fish and hunt well, but they never ventured into the darkness. They did not know if lazy Moon would come up that night or not. Moon was so unpredictable. Sometimes he rose, and sometimes he would not wake up at all.

T'kope always followed his brother into the forest, even though it made him uneasy. Klale found the cool woods soothing. Sometimes, **Raven** would lead the brothers down a long, winding trail just to tease T'kope. Raven knew Klale was a great hunter and would never get lost. T'kope worried about the **Wild Man of the Woods**, who hid in the shadows and could make the earth quake by stomping his big feet.

As the boys grew older they became inseparable. Wherever one walked, the other followed. On the beach T'kope always took the lead. This is where he felt comfortable. The smell of the salt air and the open ocean made T'kope feel free. But Klale worried about the unknown world of the sea, and when the dark of night fell, they would both rush home to the light of the fire.

One brisk morning, pulling their dugout canoe down to the shore, T'kope called out to Klale,

"Come! Today could be the day we catch the great Codfish!" Raven watched.

Fishing was good. Many gave their life to the fish box. Klale wanted to go back, but T'kope was not ready. "We must bring home the giant Codfish!" he shouted into the wind. The sea became angry at his greed and pushed the small vessel farther out to sea. Suddenly, darkness was upon them.

As the sea tossed the canoe about, Klale saw a giant monster emerge from the deep and called out to T'kope, "Take hold! There is danger about!" But T'kope did not see the monstrosity. When the next wave swelled, **Devilfish** devoured the canoe, throwing Klale adrift and pulling T'kope under.

That night, Moon slept in again. Klale was alone and far from land. Fortunately, Killer Whale, the Sea Brother of the Wolf, arrived to help Klale reach shore.

Meanwhile, Devilfish carefully placed T'kope, who was unconscious, on the back of Sea Raven, then swam away. When T'kope finally opened his eyes, he was looking at Sea Raven. "Your duty calls," Raven said. Flying through the water, **Sea Raven** and T'kope arrived at a steaming sea castle. "Master, you have come," said Sea Bear, who was guarding the castle. The gate opened, and T'kope washed through.

T'kope, the bright white Sea Wolf, was greeted by many sea creatures. "Sea Wolf, you have finally come to us," they called to him. "We need your guidance," **Sea Bear** said. "With hardly any moonbeams, our wait for you has been dark and long."

Many weeks passed, and T'kope learned to love his new family. He understood their need. This was his new home. These were his people.

Back on land, Klale missed his brother and wandered along the edge of the forest during the day. He scanned the shore, searching for T'kope. At night, Klale called upon **Moon** to wake up and help find his brother, but Moon did not hear his lonely voice.

One night, Klale heard the call of his brother and joined in the song. With the two voices howling, Moon awoke, illuminating the land and the sea.

Klale saw a white Sea Wolf in the moonlight. Klale called again, and to his wonder the Sea Wolf answered in the voice of his brother, T'kope.

Raven pulled the clouds from the north, and the light was gone. Days passed and Klale did not see his brother.

Raven stayed with Klale. When they were on the hunt, Klale did not miss his brother so much. One day, he stepped out of the forest and came to the edge of the sea. Raven followed. Gazing through the liquid surface, he saw his brother's face looking up.

Raven lifted the edge of the sea, and Klale stepped under to embrace his long-lost brother. The water fell, and they were both swept out to sea. Klale could not keep up with his Sea Wolf brother. T'kope asked his friend Bullhead to give Klale a ride.

T'kope took Klale to his new kingdom under the sea. Sea Bear and T'kope's new family were there to greet the brother of their new master. Klale saw a flash and was filled with terror. It was the **Lost Man of the Sea!** Although his brother was at home in this world, Klale was not.

T'kope wanted to share his kingdom with Klale. He thought that if he showed him all the wonders of the sea, Klale would choose to stay. But Klale was not happy. No matter how much T'kope begged his brother to stay, Klale could not say yes. He asked **Bullhead** to take him back to the world above.

T'kope followed Klale to the shore to say goodbye. Raven was there and raised the edge of the water. Raven heard Klale say to his brother, "We must come together often." The brothers of the Wolf made a promise: "We will join our voices every month." With those words, T'kope dove back into the ocean and Klale stepped out onto the land.

Klale's heart felt warm, knowing his brother
T'kope was happy and at home under the sea. The
smell of smoke from his family's fire drifted down the
beach, and he could hear the laughter of the children.
Hummingbird and all the friends from the forest
came to welcome Klale. It was good to be home.

It is said Raven released Moon
from a wooden box. That may
be true, but he could not make
Moon rise on time.

No matter where they are, the brothers of the Wolf fulfill their promise. Every month, the voice of the Wolf can be heard waking the sleeping Moon. And so, all over the world, the howl of the Wolf brings forth the light of the full Moon.

Supernatural

With no written language, the history and beliefs of the First People were passed to the next generation using art, stories, songs, and dance. They believed everything around them held a spirit within and they were connected to this spirit. This relationship between the natural world and the supernatural world influenced their way of life and their storytelling.

Bullhead is a spirit helper who often carries others on his shoulders. He also transports treasure. According to legend, Raven once squeezed Bullhead until his eyes bulged out. Bullhead managed to escape, but his eyes stayed like that. His head is broad and short with spines all around. Bullhead has thick, wide lips, and his bulging eyes are set far apart.

Devilfish is a giant octopus and a sea spirit helper who can transform into different colours and shapes. He is known to eat people, canoes, and even villages. Devilfish has eight tentacles with suckers. He has a large round head with a beak for a mouth.

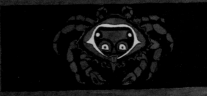

Hummingbird spends his days using love and happiness to create the coloured light that fills rainbows. In some stories, women tie Hummingbirds to their hair as adornments. Hummingbird has a long narrow beak with a small head and big eyes. He is often surrounded by flowers or rainbows.

Lost Man of the Sea is a harmless marine supernatural creature. Loon guides him from above the water. He has sea creatures attached to him and lives in an underwater kingdom. Lost Man of the Sea has big eyes and gills. He has a face like a fish and two big teeth like a beaver.

Moon was once nearly swallowed by Codfish during an eclipse, but the people built a big smoky fire, which made Codfish choke and cough Moon back into the sky. Moon and Wolf are often seen together because they both like nighttime. Moon usually has a round face with a ring around it and no rays.

Raven is a very powerful supernatural creature and a known trickster with a big appetite. It is said that Raven set Sun and Moon into the sky. He can transform himself or others into anything he wants, but in his usual form he has a long straight beak, black feathers, and wings that are usually folded by his side.

Sea Bear lives in a great kingdom under the ocean. He is a remarkable hunter who hunts Killer Whale. Sea Wolf is his friend, and they are often seen together. It is said that Sea Bear helps hold up the world. He has the head of a grizzly and the fins and tail of a whale.

Sea Raven looks similar to Raven, except he has fins like Killer Whale and lives under water. He has immense powers of transformation and likes to play tricks. Sea Raven can talk in many different voices. He can change his size and shape.

Sea Wolf is a sea monster who loves to hunt. He gathers food and takes it to his pack. Like Sea Bear, Sea Wolf can carry the world on his back. He has the head and curled tail of a wolf and the body and blowhole of a whale. He also has clawed feet and flippers.

Wild Man of the Woods is a short supernatural creature with big feet. He can stomp his feet and make the earth quake! Children fear the Wild Man of the Woods, but this fear keeps them from wandering into the forest and getting lost. He is sometimes shown as having a face like a skeleton, with big teeth and empty eye sockets.

Wolf has the greatest supernatural abilities of all animals. Wolf is a great hunter and thought to be exceptionally clever. There is a legend about a woman who, while searching for her lost sons, found two wolf cubs and brought them home. You will know Wolf by his long snout, big ears, and canine teeth. His tail is curled and he has claws.

Natural

The rich natural wonders of the Pacific Northwest Coast, including the Endeavour Segment of the Juan de Fuca Ridge, holds a collection of remarkably diverse environments and sea life. This area brings forth new discoveries every year. Young people should be encouraged to seek, discover, and protect these natural wonders.

Big Red Jellyfish are giants that grow up to three metres in diameter. They are dark red in colour and found in the Pacific Ocean. They were discovered in 2003. Instead of tentacles to capture food, like most jellyfish, Big Reds have thick, fleshy arms with a mouth on each end.

Clawed Armhook Squid live their days in water so deep, it is completely dark. During the night, they come up toward the surface of the ocean and feed by starlight. These squid have curved arms with hooks and claws on each one. Females lay two thousand to three thousand eggs in a sack coloured with black ink.

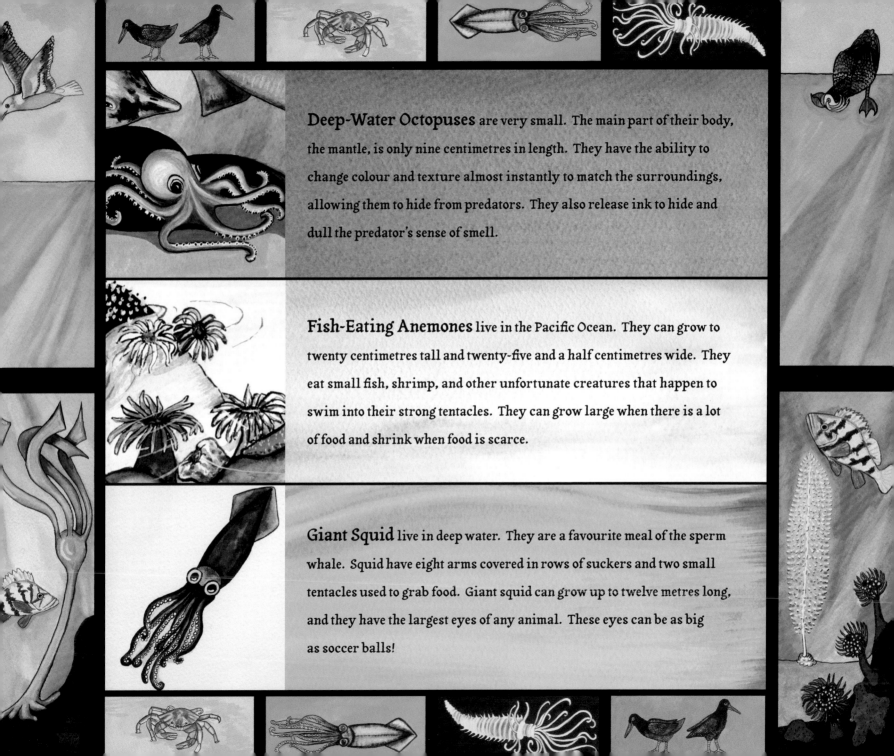

Deep-Water Octopuses are very small. The main part of their body, the mantle, is only nine centimetres in length. They have the ability to change colour and texture almost instantly to match the surroundings, allowing them to hide from predators. They also release ink to hide and dull the predator's sense of smell.

Fish-Eating Anemones live in the Pacific Ocean. They can grow to twenty centimetres tall and twenty-five and a half centimetres wide. They eat small fish, shrimp, and other unfortunate creatures that happen to swim into their strong tentacles. They can grow large when there is a lot of food and shrink when food is scarce.

Giant Squid live in deep water. They are a favourite meal of the sperm whale. Squid have eight arms covered in rows of suckers and two small tentacles used to grab food. Giant squid can grow up to twelve metres long, and they have the largest eyes of any animal. These eyes can be as big as soccer balls!

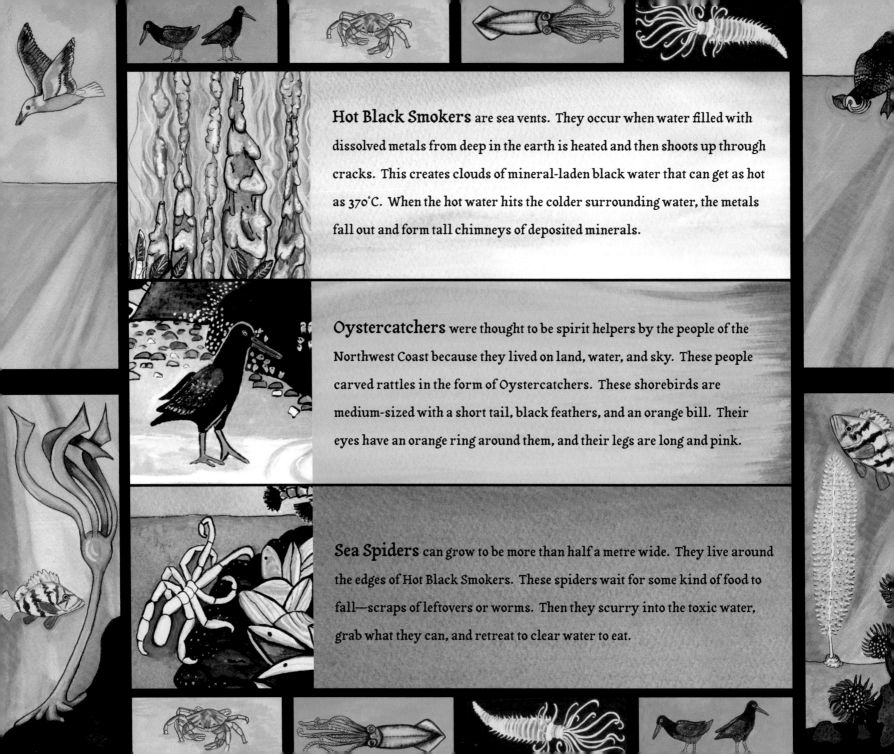

Hot Black Smokers are sea vents. They occur when water filled with dissolved metals from deep in the earth is heated and then shoots up through cracks. This creates clouds of mineral-laden black water that can get as hot as 370°C. When the hot water hits the colder surrounding water, the metals fall out and form tall chimneys of deposited minerals.

Oystercatchers were thought to be spirit helpers by the people of the Northwest Coast because they lived on land, water, and sky. These people carved rattles in the form of Oystercatchers. These shorebirds are medium-sized with a short tail, black feathers, and an orange bill. Their eyes have an orange ring around them, and their legs are long and pink.

Sea Spiders can grow to be more than half a metre wide. They live around the edges of Hot Black Smokers. These spiders wait for some kind of food to fall—scraps of leftovers or worms. Then they scurry into the toxic water, grab what they can, and retreat to clear water to eat.

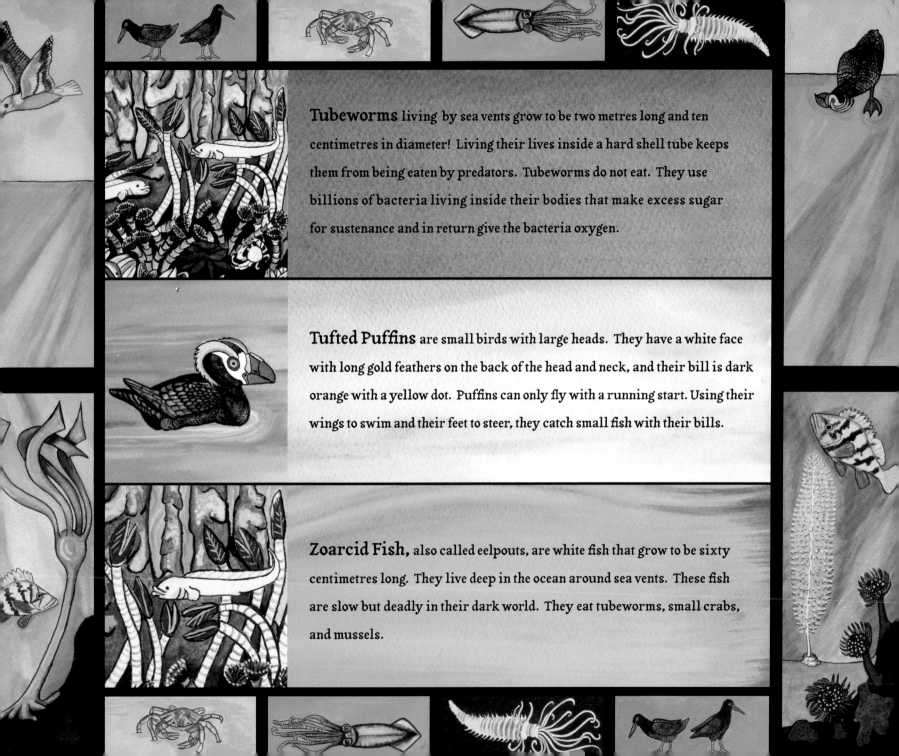

Tubeworms living by sea vents grow to be two metres long and ten centimetres in diameter! Living their lives inside a hard shell tube keeps them from being eaten by predators. Tubeworms do not eat. They use billions of bacteria living inside their bodies that make excess sugar for sustenance and in return give the bacteria oxygen.

Tufted Puffins are small birds with large heads. They have a white face with long gold feathers on the back of the head and neck, and their bill is dark orange with a yellow dot. Puffins can only fly with a running start. Using their wings to swim and their feet to steer, they catch small fish with their bills.

Zoarcid Fish, also called eelpouts, are white fish that grow to be sixty centimetres long. They live deep in the ocean around sea vents. These fish are slow but deadly in their dark world. They eat tubeworms, small crabs, and mussels.

Heritage House Publishing Company Ltd.
heritagehouse.ca

Library and Archives Canada Cataloguing in Publication

Simpson, Caroll, 1951–, author, illustrator
    Brothers of the wolf / written and illustrated by Caroll Simpson.

Issued in print and electronic formats.
ISBN 978-1-927527-96-2 (bound)
ISBN 978-1-772030-38-9 (pbk.)
ISBN 978-1-927527-97-9 (html)
ISBN 978-1-927527-98-6 (pdf)

    I. Title.

PS8637.I484B76 2014   jC813'.6   C2014-903461-X   C2014-903462-8

Edited by Lara Kordic
Proofread by Karla Decker
Cover and book design by Chyla Cardinal and Jacqui Thomas

This book was produced using FSC®-certified, acid-free paper, processed chlorine free and printed with vegetable-based inks.

Heritage House acknowledges the financial support for its publishing program from the Government of Canada through the Canada Book Fund (CBF), Canada Council for the Arts, and the Province of British Columbia through the British Columbia Arts Council and the Book Publishing Tax Credit.

Canadian Heritage   Patrimoine canadien
Canada Council for the Arts   Conseil des Arts du Canada
BRITISH COLUMBIA ARTS COUNCIL   Supported by the Province of British Columbia

18 17 16 15 14 1 2 3 4 5

Printed in Canada

AUTHOR'S NOTE

My goal in writing this book is to enhance children's understanding of the peoples who were here before European contact. I did not retell a First Nations legend. Rather, I wrote my own story of two wolf brothers who accept their differences and follow their own paths, and I threaded into the story traits common to the supernatural creatures and beings of Northwest Coast mythologies. I also incorporated flora and fauna of the northwestern Pacific Ocean. I hope this book will inspire young readers of all ethnicities to further their knowledge of and respect for all First Nations culture, art, history, and mythology, as well as the wonders of the northwestern Pacific Ocean.

Many sources inspired me, including the following:

Hilary Stewart's *Looking at Indian Art of the Northwest Coast* (Douglas & McIntyre, 2004) and *Looking at Totem Poles* (Douglas & McIntyre, 1993). Stewart's books are always by my side. She delivers clear and precise identification methods and mythologies and understands Northwest Coast art.

Indian Myths and Legends from the North Pacific Coast of America: Translation from Franz Boas' 1895 Edition of Indianische Sagen von der Nord-Pacifischen Küste Amerikas (Talonbooks, 2006). Franz Boas wrote volumes about the First People, including many meticulously documented legends. We are fortunate to have access to these old records.

Bill Reid and Bill Holm's *Indian Art of the Northwest Coast: A Dialogue on Craftsmanship and Aesthetics* (University of Washington Press, 1975).

Bill Holm's *Northwest Coast Indian Art: An Analysis of Form* (University of Washington Press, 1965). Bill Holm has assembled criteria for anyone working in the Northwest Coast artistic tradition.

Cheryl Shearar's *Understanding Northwest Coast Art: A Guide to Crests, Beings and Symbols* (Douglas & McIntyre, 2000). Shearar's interpretation of First Nations art, legends, and traits is an excellent compendium.

Pat Kramer's *Totem Poles* (Heritage House, 2008). A colourful, informative collection of historic totems that includes legends, descriptions, and locations.

Glenn Bartley's *Birds of British Columbia: A Photographic Journey* (Heritage House, 2013). A comprehensive guide to BC birds.

Andy Lamb and Bernard Hanby's *Marine Life of the Pacific Northwest: A Photographic Encyclopedia of Invertebrates, Seaweeds and Selected Fishes* (Harbour Publishing, 2005).

Articles on the Endeavour Segment of the Juan de Fuca Ridge:

UBC Department of Geography, "Endeavour Hypothermal Vents," geog.ubc.ca/biodiversity/EndeavourHotVents.html.

Fisheries and Oceans Canada, "Endeavour Hydrothermal Vents," dfo-mpo.gc.ca/oceans/marineareas-zonesmarines/mpa-zpm/pacific-pacifique/factsheets-feuillets/endeavour-eng.htm.

The Oceanography Society, "Endeavour Segment of the Juan de Fuca Ridge," *Oceanography* 25, no. 1, 2012, tos.org/oceanography/archive/25-1_kelley.pdf.